P9-DND-605

One Small Dog

One Small Dog

BY JOHANNA HURWITZ

ILLUSTRATED BY DIANE DE GROAT

HarperCollins*Publishers*

In memory of Sinbad and Selena

One Small Dog
Text copyright © 2000 by Johanna Hurwitz
Illustrations copyright © 2000 by Diane deGroat
1350 Avenue of the Americas, New York, NY 10019,
or visit our website at www.harperchildrens.com.

Library of Congress Cataloging-in-Publication Data
Hurwitz, Johanna.
One small dog / by Johanna Hurwitz; illustrated by Diane de Groat.
p. cm.
Summary: Curtis gets a dog when his parents divorce, but his beloved new
dog causes problems that he did not expect.
ISBN 0-688-17382-9 (trade)—ISBN 0-06-029220-2 (library)
[1. Dogs—Fiction.   2. Divorce—Fiction.]   I. de Groat, Diane, ill.   II. Title.
PZ7.H9574 Op 2000   [Fic]—dc21   99-87073

Typography by Robbin Gourley
1   2   3   4   5   6   7   8   9   10
❖
First Edition

Contents

1

The Bad News and the Good

I started biting my nails the spring that I was in fourth grade. My schoolwork got worse and worse then too. Finally, after a couple of warnings, my teacher, Mrs. Richmond, phoned my mom to set up a conference.

Afterward Mom said, "Mrs. Richmond didn't know about the divorce."

"It's not something I go around talking about," I told her.

"Maybe not. But she said that under the circumstances it explained your behavior."

I shrugged my shoulders. What could I

say? My whole life changed on the night before the night before Christmas, when my parents told Mitchell and me the news that they were getting divorced. Mitch didn't understand. How could he? He's only three years old. When he heard that we'd be moving to a new apartment, he thought it would be fun. After all, he didn't have a good friend living two floors above. Mitch also liked the idea of visiting Dad on the weekends and eating frozen dinners, which is all Dad knows how to cook. The news didn't upset Mitchell at all.

Of course, after I heard about the divorce, Christmas was really lousy. My dad hadn't moved out yet, but he kept out of the way. Also, when I looked at the computer games that I had asked for as presents, I realized that now they would be useless. Dad was sure to take the computer with him when he moved. I knew it was pretty dumb to be upset about the computer, but if I thought about that, I didn't have to think about my dad and mom splitting up.

At first when I heard about the divorce, I kept hoping it was only temporary. I remembered when one of the girls in my class named Jessie came to school in tears because her parents had split up. Then, a few weeks later, she came in all excited and with good news. They had gotten back together again. That could happen in my family too, I thought. But it didn't.

Right after the New Year, Dad moved out. He sublet an apartment way downtown, and just as I thought, he took the computer and some of our furniture with him. It seemed strange to be living with just Mom and Mitch. Life was a whole lot quieter without the loud jazz music that my father listened to all the time. And no yelling or screaming going on.

Thinking back, I realized my parents rarely spoke to each other. They just yelled all the time. I know that lots of parents fight. I've heard it when I've gone to visit my friends. Once when I was staying over at Josh Bumpus's house for supper, I saw Josh's mother throw a plateful of tuna noodle casserole on the floor when his father complained that he didn't want to eat that slop. I was amazed. But then Josh's mother started laughing, and his father helped clean up the mess. Afterward Josh's father ate two servings of tuna noodle casserole to prove that he was sorry.

My mom never threw a plateful of food on the floor, but she never started laughing with my dad in the middle of a fight either.

The good news was that even though we moved, I didn't have to change schools. But I did have to share my bedroom with Mitchell. What's worse, at Dad's apartment, I had to share more than a bedroom. Mitch and I slept together on a pullout sofa. And just between you and me, even though Mitch has been toilet trained for the last year, he still has accidents at night.

After we moved, Mitch began having accidents all the time. Even during the day. And when we went to spend the weekend with Dad, Mitch cried when we left Mom. Then he cried again when Dad brought us back home.

I knew just how he felt. Lots of times I wanted to cry too. But when you're almost ten years old, it's not cool to act like a baby. So I didn't cry, but I guess that's when I began biting my nails.

I never saw my mom cry either. But sometimes her eyes were red when she woke up in the morning. And once when we were sitting together watching a video, she began wiping her eyes.

"What's the matter?" I asked her as she blew her nose into a tissue.

It felt strange seeing her tears.

"This is a sad movie," she said. Well, it was

a little sad. But I don't think that was why she was crying.

Gradually, though, my mom seemed to become more cheerful. She said our new apartment, which was the top floor of an old brownstone house owned by friends of hers, had more character than the modern high-rise building we had left behind. She cut down our old curtains to fit the new windows and seemed to enjoy moving the furniture and deciding the best place for those pieces that she had kept for herself.

Our apartment might have had *charm*, but it sure was small. There were just two bedrooms, and even though Mitch and I shared the larger one, it was smaller than the room I used to have to myself.

Mitch was always underfoot. I'd be doing my homework, and he would push my arm, making me mess up my paper.

"What you doing?" he always wanted to know.

"Math."

"What's math?" he asked me.

"You'll find out when you grow up."

"When's that?"

He was driving me bananas. I never had a minute of privacy. Now that we were on top of each other, I found myself yelling at him a lot. It sounded as if we were headed for a breakup too. But kids can't divorce their younger brothers.

I was also upset because I saw my friend Danny only at school. Before we moved, Danny and I did our homework together and sometimes had supper at each other's houses. Now it became a big deal if we wanted to get together. But I guess the worst thing for me was that I never had any special time alone with Dad. I used to look forward to the times when the two of us went together to basketball games at Madison Square Garden. Now I saw Dad only on the weekend. We went to places like the zoo or to kiddie movies that

Mitchell liked. It was boring.

No wonder I was so unhappy.

"Divorce is hard," my mother said. "But you'll get used to it in time. Do you know that half the couples in the United States are getting divorced these days? Still, life goes on."

"Yeah," I said. "But it stinks. Why couldn't we be part of the half that stays together?" I wanted to say more, but I was afraid I'd start crying.

Mom put her arms around me. "I also wanted to be part of the half that stays together," she said, sniffing.

I pulled away. If she started crying, I knew I would too.

"Come on," she said, trying to smile. "Think of something that would cheer you up. When you were little, it was a lollipop. What would make you happy now?"

I suppose I could have asked for my own computer, but I needed something more than that. It would take more than a machine to make me feel better. Suddenly I had a brilliant idea. This was my chance!

"A dog!" I told my mom. "I want a dog."

"Oh, Curtis, that's crazy," she said at once. "You know I've always said a dog doesn't belong in a city apartment. And now we're living in even less space than ever."

"We could get a small dog," I said hopefully.

"How about a tankful of fish?" she replied.

"Fish!" I exploded. "Fish are for supper. Not for a pet! You can't play with them or walk them or love them," I added.

I've wanted a dog since I started talking. My first words, even before *Mama* and *Dada*, were *wow wow*. My mom says that whenever I saw a dog, I began screaming, "Wow wow." So they gave me a stuffed toy dog and a pull-toy dog with wheels. But as soon as I could speak in full sentences, I asked for the real thing. The answer was always the same: *No.*

So I don't know why I thought now would be different. Still, I had a shred of hope.

"What would happen on the weekends when you aren't here?" my mom asked.

I jumped up with excitement. From her tone and from the question, I suddenly knew I was going to get a dog after all.

"I'll take him to Dad's," I said. "You won't have to do anything. I'll walk him, I'll feed him, I'll do everything. And I'll be so happy."

"Well . . . ," my mother said, sighing.

"Say yes," I begged.

Mom looked at me and smiled. "You win," she said. "But I probably should have my head examined for giving in."

I threw my arms around her and gave her a big hug. These days I hardly ever hug her. It seems too babyish a thing to do. But at that moment no one was happier than me. I was going to get a dog!

2

A Dog Called Sammy

From the minute I knew I was going to get a dog, I felt like a new person. I offered to read aloud to Mitch, and I even sat on the floor and helped him build with his blocks.

Of course I was still sorry about my parents and the divorce, but for once I didn't lie in bed that night thinking about them. Also, the heavy feeling that had been pressing inside me seemed to melt away. Now I had something else to think about.

What would I name my dog? I'd met many dogs with food names like Cookie and Peanuts and Licorice. I also knew of dogs with names that described them: Blackie, Boots (who had white paws), and Tiny. Tiny was just that, a chihuahua that belonged to a girl in my first-grade class named Amanda. She brought the dog to school for show-and-tell.

One thing I knew for sure: Much as I wanted a dog, I didn't want a chihuahua. I remembered how Amanda's dog shivered and shook all the time and how she barked with a high, yelping sound that was awful. Sure, I'd told Mom I'd get a small dog, but not a tiny one.

I decided that the best name for a dog would be a real people kind of name. I would name my dog Charlie or Roger or Michael. After all, I knew my dog was going to be my new best friend.

When I spoke to my dad on the phone the next evening, I told him the big news.

"Hey, pal, you don't want a dog," he said. "You're just going to make your life more complicated. You'll have to rush home from school to walk it. Believe me, having a dog isn't what you think it is."

Of course I didn't believe him at all. I *wanted* to have a dog waiting for me to walk him.

"Put your mom on the phone," Dad said. "I can't take you and Mitch this weekend. I have to attend an out-of-town conference for work, and I'll be away until Tuesday."

I was sorry that I wouldn't see my father, but when Mom said we'd go to the animal shelter on Saturday, I was happy about the change in plans.

For Mitch, the animal shelter was a new zoo that he'd never been to before. Of course there were no lions and tigers or seals and monkeys. Instead we saw a huge room full of kittens and cats and another, noisier one filled with dogs of every size, color, and species. The shelter was crowded with people who, like me, were looking for pets to adopt. I wasn't the only one searching for the perfect dog. There seemed to be enough animals to go around, but I hoped that I got the one I wanted and someone didn't beat me to him.

At first I didn't know which way to look. I started toward a cage nearby.

"A *little* dog," my mom said in her how-in-the-world-did-I-get-myself-in-this-situation voice. She pushed me in the opposite direction, where there was a cage holding smaller animals.

"This zoo smells," Mitchell complained, holding on to his nose.

He was right. It stank. Any other day I would automatically have responded to my brother by saying, "It smells like you when you wet the bed!" But I didn't feel like making mean cracks at Mitchell when I was so busy checking out dogs. And I was too happy and excited to let the stinky odor of the animal shelter bother me. A single small dog in our apartment wouldn't smell like that.

There were six dogs in the cage near where I was standing. I put my fingers through the holes in the mesh that covered the cages and tried to touch the dogs. Some of the animals hung back timidly while others rubbed up against the mesh. One dog came over and touched my fingers with his cold, wet nose. Then he licked my fingers with his bright pink tongue. It tickled.

"Hi, fella," I said to him. "Do you like me?"

The dog had curly black fur and floppy ears. His tail wagged back and forth as he kept licking my hand.

"Look, Mom," I called. "Here's one that really likes me."

"Did you wash your hands after breakfast?" she asked. "He may like you, but I bet he likes the bacon you ate this morning even more."

"You like *me*, don't you?" I asked the dog again.

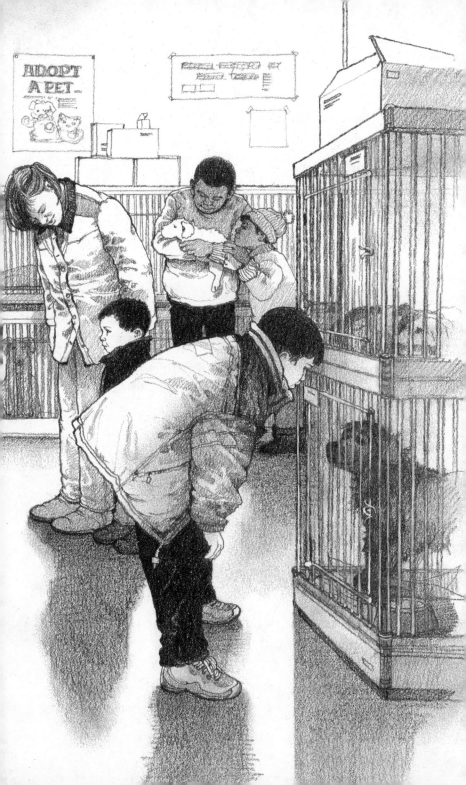

Mom smiled. "He does seem friendly," she admitted. "Let me ask the attendant about him."

There were two people working in the dog room of the animal shelter, and both were busy helping other people. I began to worry that someone else would try to claim the black dog. I reached into the cage with my other hand, and while the dog licked the fingers of my right hand, I stroked his dark hair with the fingers of my left hand.

"Nice doggy," said Mitchell, taking his hand off his nose.

"See. Even Mitch likes him," I said.

"He's not too big," my mom said.

I smiled at her. "He's perfect," I said, lowering my voice. I didn't want anyone else to hear about this special dog until he officially belonged to me.

Suddenly, standing there petting the black dog, I knew what I was going to name him. "Sammy," I whispered to him. "Your name is

Sammy." Sam Eisenberg, who had curly black hair just like this dog's, had been my first real friend back in kindergarten and first grade. But then his family had moved away, and I saw him only one more time, when I was invited for a sleepover at his new house in Connecticut. I still think about him sometimes, and it would be great to have another friend named Sammy.

At last my mother was able to get the attention of one of the animal shelter workers. The woman opened the cage and picked up the black dog. Finally I could really touch Sammy and even put my arm around him. Sammy seemed to understand what was going on. His tail was wagging like crazy, but he didn't try to jump out of the woman's arms.

"He seems quite tame?" my mom said as though she were asking a question rather than stating a fact.

"This dog is just twelve weeks old," the woman said. She wore a tag with her name on it: Libby. "He's part cocker spaniel and part mutt," she said. "He's very docile," she said, looking down at the dog in her arms. "He'll probably be very gentle. Good with children," she added, nodding toward Mitchell.

Mitch is kind of shy around dogs. But he reached up cautiously and touched the dog's back. The dog turned his head, and his pink tongue came out and licked Mitch's hand for a moment. Mitch pulled back his hand fearfully.

"He's kissing you," Libby told him.

Mitchell began giggling. He'd never been kissed by a dog before. "Nice doggy," he said, but he backed away.

"How big will this dog get?" asked Mom.

"I think he's going to stay rather small," said Libby. We followed her as she led us out of the noisy, smelly dog room and into the area where we had to fill out adoption forms.

"I didn't realize it was so complicated to get a dog," my mom said. "All these papers.

You'd think we were taking a child."

"Animals must be treated with the same respect as humans," Libby told Mom.

"Sammy's very important," I reassured Libby. "We'll take extra-good care of him."

"Sammy?" the woman asked. Then she realized that it was the dog's new name. "Good," she said. "I'm sure you can do it. It takes love and patience. Just like with a young child."

"I'm a young child," said Mitch proudly.

"Yes, you are. Don't grab the dog's tail or pull his hair."

"I won't," Mitch said, reaching out cautiously to touch the tip of Sammy's tail. "I'll be very gentle."

Even though the dog would belong to me, it was my mother who had to fill out the forms and sign her name. "You're considered too young," my mom explained when I said it didn't seem right. Mom also wrote a check to cover the adoption fees, and in return she was given several papers about dog care and a sample bag of dog food. Libby attached a canvas leash to Sammy's collar and handed him to me.

"Good luck," she said as she turned to go back to help the next person who was going to adopt a dog.

We had taken the subway to get to the animal shelter. But we had to take a taxicab back home. "Only guide dogs belonging to blind people are permitted to travel on the subway or bus," my mother explained. I'd never thought about that before.

Sammy sat on my lap and looked out the window just like Mitch. I couldn't take my eyes off my dog. His mouth was open, and his pink tongue hung out. I could see his white teeth. They looked so clean, as if he'd brushed them after breakfast, the way I was supposed to do but had forgotten. His claws dug into my jeans, but they didn't hurt. I breathed in the doggy smell of his fur. It was wonderful. After waiting all my life, I finally had a dog. There was no doubt in my mind that I had gotten the very best dog in the whole animal shelter. Then it occurred to me that at least one good thing had come out of my parents' divorce. When they lived together, they both had agreed that I couldn't have a dog. Actually it was one of the few things they had agreed on.

3

"Welcome Home"

"This is your new home!" I announced proudly to Sammy as we entered our apartment.

He ran around and around, sniffing in all the corners, squeezing under the sofa in case there was something of interest for a dog, and in general checking out what our place looked like. I think he approved. He kept wagging his tail, and he looked happy. If I had a tail, I'd have been wagging it too.

But right from the start there were little problems. To begin with, Sammy needed to be housebroken. So that first Saturday I must have walked him a dozen times. It was fun, walking along the street holding on to the leash and showing him off to anyone I saw. I'd phoned my friend Danny to see if he could meet me, but he wasn't home.

Whenever Sammy spotted another dog, he began barking and took off toward him and pulled me along. Luckily I'd twisted the leash around my hand or I might have lost him more than once. Instead I practically dislocated my arm from the yank of the leash.

"Hey, slow down," I shouted to my dog. "You didn't act that way at the shelter."

Most of the other dogs we saw were twice Sammy's size. One huge dog gave a bark or two that quieted my dog. Its owner was a man who hardly paid any attention to us and just kept on walking. Maybe after a while I'd be able to keep Sammy under control the way the man had done with his dog.

I felt a little silly watching to be sure my dog made puddles. But I was also watching for the big stuff. I knew Mom would have a fit if Sammy made a mess in our apartment.

When we ate lunch, Sammy ran around the kitchen table begging for food.

Mitch sat on his chair looking scared. I think he was waiting for Sammy to steal the frankfurter off his plate.

"Here, Sammy," I said, biting off a piece and offering it to him.

"No, you don't," my mom said, stopping me. "The booklet says to feed your dog just twice a day, in the morning and in the evening."

"I'm happy I get lunch," Mitch said.

I felt that way too. I was sure the shelter had made a mistake. How could a dog eat just two meals a day?

Luckily for Sammy, Mitch accidentally dropped half his frank on the floor. Sammy gobbled up the bread and meat before my mother or I could grab it from him. I have to admit I didn't try very hard. It seemed to me that Sammy deserved any food he could get hold of.

"Well, you won't have to do much cleaning anymore," I said. Sammy was sniffing all the corners of the room looking for another bite to eat.

That evening Mom had a hard time cooking supper because Sammy stood at her heels as she dipped the chicken pieces into bread crumbs. When she bent with the pan of chicken to place it inside the oven, Sammy almost managed to grab one of the legs.

"Curtis! Get this dog out of here!" she yelled at me.

"Come here, Sammy," I called to my dog. But much as he liked me, he liked food a whole lot more.

When it was suppertime, Sammy finally got his own meal. Mom poured out two cups of the dog food that we'd been given at the shelter and added water.

"I want cereal for supper too," said Mitch.

"That's not cereal, dummy," I told him. "It's puppy chow."

"Curtis, don't speak to your brother like that," Mom said.

"It looks like cereal to me," Mitch insisted.

Actually he was right. The dog food did look like some sort of cold breakfast cereal. Sammy gulped it down so fast that I figured he must be starving.

"He needs more," I told my mother.

"Nope," she said. She held up the instruction sheet. "One portion at supper. And one at breakfast time."

Mom found Sammy so annoying at suppertime that she locked him in the bedroom I shared with Mitch. He whined and barked all through the meal. Much as I like chicken, I didn't have much appetite listening to Sammy's cries. "He's still hungry," I kept saying.

At bedtime Mom thought Sammy should spend the night in the kitchen.

"You're really going to confuse him," I protested. "First you lock him up in the bedroom to keep him out of the kitchen. Then you want to put him in the kitchen and keep him out of the bedroom."

I nagged at Mom until she gave in. Sammy could sleep on the rug in the bedroom, she said.

Mitch was already asleep, with his head resting against his teddy bear, when Sammy and I came into the bedroom. He jumped up on my bed immediately.

"Get him down," my mother said.

"Down, Sammy. Down," I said, picking him up and placing him on the floor. But when the door was closed and the light was off and I felt him jump up on the bed, I didn't say a word. He walked around on the bed and licked my face when he found it. I reached up and patted him. "Good dog," I whispered, even though if my mother had seen us, she would have been shouting just the opposite.

Sammy moved around until he found a comfortable spot. He lay down and fell asleep even before I did. I felt so cozy and happy inside, feeling his body moving with his breaths.

In the middle of the night I turned over and felt a soft, warm bump with my foot. It took me a moment to remember. It was my dog!

On the weekends I like to stay in bed late to make up for going off to school so early the rest of the week. Sammy must have wakened quite a while before I did because in the morning when I finally focused my eyes, the first thing I saw was my dog chewing away on one of my sneakers. I would never have guessed his teeth were sharp enough to do all the damage he had done. The rubber surrounding the toe was in shreds.

Mitch was awake and was sitting and watching the whole thing with as much fascination as if it were a TV cartoon.

"What does a sneaker taste like?" he wanted to know.

"I guess it tastes different to a dog from the way it would to us," I replied, watching Sammy's obvious enjoyment.

"Like candy?" Mitch asked.

"Maybe. Or a steak."

I got out of bed and immediately began searching in the closet for my old sneaks. They were getting tight on me, but I wasn't about to complain. I took the ruined sneaker and the other one of the pair and hid them far in the back of the closet. I knew my mom wouldn't be pleased to see them. They were only a couple of weeks old.

"Come on, Sammy," I called to him as soon as I was dressed. "Let's go take a walk."

"I want to come too," Mitch said, now that his entertainment was over.

"It's early," I told him. "Wait till later. I'll be taking Sammy for a lot more walks today."

"Okay," he said.

My sneaker was just the beginning. Sammy chewed up both of my mother's bedroom slippers while she was at work on Monday. Two of Mitch's stuffed toys were destroyed on Tuesday. And before the week was out, Sammy would ruin a scarf of my mother's, which had fallen on the floor.

"It's our fault," I said, defending Sammy. "We shouldn't leave anything on the floor. He's teething, and he needs to chew."

"What about the sofa leg?" my mother asked. "Even if we pick up the magazines and toys and slippers, how do we keep the furniture out of his range?"

"He's probably hungry too," I said. "How would you like to get only two meals a day and both of them that dry stuff we feed him?"

"I wouldn't like it," Mom said. "But he seems to love every single piece. Look at how quickly he devours it each time."

"That's because he's starving."

Then it was Wednesday. What happened on Wednesday was also because the poor dog was hungry.

4

What Happened
on Wednesday

Wednesday started out as a usual day. As soon as I woke, I had to jump out of bed and get dressed quickly so I could take Sammy for his early-morning walk. When we came back, I poured out Sammy's bowl of puppy food and gave him some fresh water to drink. Then I had to swallow my orange juice and gobble up some toast really fast, grab my backpack, and rush off to catch the bus to school.

Mom and Mitch left a few minutes later. Mom drops Mitch off at the day-care center, and then she goes on to work.

Like most days, on Wednesday I got home first.

As I walked up the stairs leading to our apartment, Mrs. Hoffman, who lives below us, stopped me on the landing. "I've been out all day," she told me. "And when I came in, I heard a strange banging noise. It's coming from your apartment."

I stood on the landing and listened. "I don't hear anything," I told her.

"It comes and goes. I can't figure out what it is," she said. "I don't think it's the water pipes. I also seemed to be the only person in the building, so I couldn't ask the Hendersons to check it out."

Midge and Alfred Henderson are the friends of my mother's who own the building.

As she spoke, there was a banging sound.

"There it goes again," said our neighbor. "Maybe I should go upstairs with you."

I looked at Mrs. Hoffman. She's about twice my mom's age and twice her weight too.

I wondered what help she'd be if the pipes were acting up or if there was another sort of problem.

"That's all right," I said. "I'll figure out what's going on."

The banging got louder as I reached our door. It was as if someone were inside the apartment and trying to get out. But I knew no one was home. No one but Sammy.

I admit I was a little bit scared as I turned the key in the lock and opened the door. In front of my eyes was a sight that made me start laughing. It was like something out of a TV comedy. The hind legs of my dog were moving around, but his head was stuck inside an antique metal milk can that my mother kept in the entranceway.

For some dumb reason Sammy had put his head inside. Now he couldn't get out. It looked awfully funny, but I realized it wasn't something to laugh about.

I threw down my backpack and went to his

rescue. "Hold still, Sammy," I told him as I grabbed hold of his back legs. I tried to brace the milk can with my feet as I pulled on Sammy.

I heard a muffled bark from the dog, but he was still stuck inside.

While I was trying to figure out what to do next, the doorbell rang. "It's me, Mrs. Hoffman," a breathless voice called out. "Is everything all right?"

I let go of Sammy's hindquarters and went to open the door.

"Oh, my heavens!" my neighbor exclaimed.

"I'm not sure how he got in. And I'm not sure how he's going to get out," I said as we both stared at the part of poor Sammy that wasn't inside the milk can.

"Dial nine-one-one," said Mrs. Hoffman.

"The police?" Why would you call the police? It was pretty awful, but it wasn't a crime.

"No, wait," said Mrs. Hoffman, hurrying over to our phone. "We should call the fire department. You know how people call them if a cat gets stuck up a tree."

She began punching in the numbers for the fire department. I was glad she was doing it because I felt sure if I did it, I'd get in trouble for making a false alarm. Besides, didn't people call the fire department when cats were up in trees because there were tall ladders at the firehouse? For sure, one thing we didn't need here was a tall ladder.

I listened as Mrs. Hoffman tried to explain to the person on the line just what the problem was. "It's not a big emergency. Just a small one," she said.

It *was* a big emergency if you were Sammy, I thought. Poor Sammy kept banging the milk can on the floor. I wondered if he'd be stuck inside forever. I felt so helpless, but I kept patting his rear, just so he'd know I was there.

Believe it or not, the fire department actually sent a truck to our building. It arrived just as Mom and Mitch did. Mitch was thrilled to see a big fire engine at our front door. Worried that the house was on fire, Mom came rushing up the stairs with him. I don't know if she was relieved or not when she saw what the problem was.

In the end it took three firefighters and four-foot-long bolt cutters to free poor Sammy from that metal milk can.

When the can was cut away, we discovered that it had been the storage place for every piece of food that Mitch hadn't wanted to eat during recent weeks—half sandwiches, a chunk of banana, even a couple of cookies. No wonder my poor, always-hungry dog had stuck his head inside the milk can.

"Sorry we had to destroy this can," the firefighter who cut it open apologized to Mom.

"It was either that or have an awfully noisy

dog on our hands," she said, shaking her head.

"Was it very valuable?" I asked her. I thought I'd probably have to hand over my allowance for the next ten years to pay for that old milk can.

Mom shrugged her shoulders. "Who knows?" she said. "Your father and I picked it up in New Hampshire on our honeymoon. I think it's very symbolic that it's been destroyed."

I wasn't sure what she meant by that, but at least she wasn't angry.

As for Sammy, he was so happy to be free that he ran around and around. I hugged him and thought, Wait till I get to school tomorrow. No one's going to believe this story. I could hardly believe it myself!

5

Trouble on Thursday

That evening I called my father. Sometimes when we speak on the phone,
neither of us has much to say. But that night
I had loads to tell him. Because he'd been
away, it was the first time I'd spoken with
him since I'd gotten Sammy. Of course I told
him all about my wonderful new dog. I also
described the crazy afternoon we'd just had
with the firefighters and all.

"Wait till you see Sammy," I told Dad. "I'll
bring him when Mitch and I come to visit on
Friday."

"Wait a minute, pal," my dad said. "I'm
not so sure that's a good idea. I think there's
something in my lease about not having

pets in this building."

"You don't have a pet," I told him. "I do. And Sammy is just coming for a *short* visit."

"It may still be a problem."

Even though I would have hated being away from him for even two days, I might have considered leaving Sammy at home with my mother. But then I remembered how I'd promised her that she wouldn't have to take care of the dog on the weekends when I was visiting with Dad.

"I'll sneak him in," I said, thinking very quickly. "No one will even know that you have a dog visiting."

"What are you going to do? Dress him up like a kid and teach him to walk on two legs?" Dad asked. His sense of humor is not the greatest.

"Not exactly. But I'll figure out something."

I had less than two days to come up with an idea. But before that happened, there was another disaster at our house. Mom was speaking on the telephone Thursday afternoon, and Sammy jumped up and pulled a paper bag containing a pound of hamburger meat off the kitchen table. By the time Mom noticed, Sammy had eaten most of the meat and the paper bag as well. When she saw what was happening, she dropped the phone and grabbed the remaining meat away from the dog.

Sammy snarled at her and nipped her right hand with his teeth. Mom let out such a scream you would have thought he had chewed her whole arm off. "Look what that dog did to me!" she shouted.

I ran to the medicine cabinet and got the box of bandages. "It's just a little nip," I said.

"Dogs that bite can't be pets!" she said.

"Everyone knows you shouldn't take food away from an animal," I said. I don't remember where I learned that. Maybe it was on a nature program on TV.

"I can take *my* supper away from him," said Mom as she held her hand under the cold-water faucet. "It was your supper too," she added.

"Look at the clock," I said. "It's almost time for him to eat. He was hungry," I said in Sammy's defense.

Mom sighed. She put the bandage on her hand and sat down on one of the kitchen chairs. "Listen, honey," she said, putting her bandaged hand on my shoulder, "I know you love that dog. I'm growing fond of him myself, but if this sort of thing happens again, he's got to go. Do you understand? We can't have a biting dog in this house."

I could tell from her voice that she really meant it. I looked over at Sammy, who was sitting in a corner of the kitchen. It would be awful if I had to give him up. "He won't do that again. Ever," I told her.

That night we ate scrambled eggs. I didn't care. Just so Sammy could stay. He could eat my supper every night.

It wasn't until I was getting ready for bed that evening that Mom realized the telephone was still off the hook. "Well, that's one way to get rid of those pesty salespeople who always call when we sit down to eat," she said, laughing. "I wonder what that man on the phone thought when he heard me scream?"

It was good to hear Mom laughing, I thought as I got into bed. As usual Sammy waited until the light was out before jumping up on my bed. "Sammy," I whispered in the dark, "you've got to be good. Don't make my mom angry anymore, okay?" I begged him.

The last thing I remembered before I fell asleep was Sammy licking my hand. I was sure it was his way of saying that he'd behave.

6

Visiting Dad

It was on the bus, going to school on Friday, that I figured out a plan for secretly getting Sammy into Dad's apartment. What I did was borrow a large canvas tote bag that my mother sometimes used when she went off on errands in the neighborhood. It was big enough to hold several small bags if she went to more than one shop. It was also big enough to hide Sammy.

We had a practice session as soon as I returned home from school. I put Sammy in the bag and walked around our apartment so he'd get used to the motion.

Sammy thought it was a game. He kept poking his head out of the bag and giving little barks. Eventually he settled down inside, especially after I sprinkled some of his dog food in the bottom of the bag. I played the let's-take-a-walk-inside-the-bag game several times until Sammy knew his part perfectly.

Mom said she didn't like the idea of sneaking Sammy into Dad's apartment building. "You might get away with it once, but someone is bound to discover you have a dog in there," she said, pointing to her tote bag.

"Well, I want Dad to see Sammy, and I'd miss him too much if I had to leave him home," I told her. Besides, I was remembering my promise that she wouldn't have to take care of the dog on the weekends. I guess she was remembering it too, and she didn't protest.

Mitch and I always take a taxi to my dad's apartment. Mom knows just how much the fare will be plus a tip. She gives me a little extra in case we're caught in traffic and it comes to more. So later that afternoon Mitch and I, our two overnight cases, and the canvas tote bag with Sammy inside stood on the corner of our block as Mom hailed a taxi. "Call me as soon as you arrive," she told me as she does every time.

"Sure, sure," I said, climbing into the taxi carrying the tote bag with one hand and the overnight case with the other. The driver had to wait while Mitch gave my mother about seven good-bye kisses. "You act like you're never going to see her again," I commented when he finally sat down inside and Mom slammed the door shut. But at least he wasn't crying the way he usually was when we went to Dad's.

"I love her," Mitch said.

I love Mom too. But I wasn't going to do all that kissing out on the street.

"That's right," said the taxi driver, who had a long black beard and mustache. "Love your mother. No one will ever love you more.

Where to, gentlemen?"

I told him the address.

"Well, seeing as you love your mother, I guess you're not running away from home, are you?" the driver asked, looking at Mitch through the rearview mirror.

"We're going to see Daddy," Mitch responded.

"Oh," said the driver, whose name was Rabindranath Patel. It was printed under his picture for everyone to check out.

Just then Sammy popped his head out of the tote bag and gave a little bark.

"Which one of you did that?" asked Mr. Patel.

"That's Sammy," Mitch told him.

"Well, Sammy," Mr. Patel said, turning around to take a better look at me, "you're really good at animal imitations. Can you do this?" Suddenly the cab was filled with the sound of a dozen chickens.

That really got Sammy excited. Mitch was

excited too. "Do it again," he begged when Mr. Patel stopped to take a breath.

So we made it all the way to my father's apartment to the noise of chickens clucking, roosters crowing, Mitch cheering, and Sammy barking. Only I was quiet. I was worried about calming Sammy down before we tried to enter Dad's apartment building.

Luckily I had a whole bag of puppy chow inside my overnight case.

We pulled up in front of my dad's apartment house. Mr. Patel told me the fare, though I could read it perfectly clearly on the meter. "No extra charge for entertainment," he said, smiling.

"This is the best taxi we were ever in," said Mitch, delighting Mr. Patel. I gave him a tip, and he was even happier.

"Maybe I'll see you again," he said.

There are thousands of taxis in New York City, so I don't think it's very likely.

Mr. Patel turned off the motor and got out

of the cab. He came around and opened the door and helped Mitch get out with his overnight case. He wanted to help me too, but I wasn't ready to leave the safety of the taxi yet.

"Just a minute," I said, as I unzipped the overnight case and found the plastic bag of dog food. I grabbed a handful and threw it into the tote bag. Mr. Patel looked inside the bag and saw Sammy.

"I suppose you want to see all the chickens I have in the front seat too?" he asked.

For one moment he fooled me. But then I saw he was smiling. One of his teeth was made of gold. I got out of the taxi with my two bags.

"Good-bye. Good-bye." Mitch waved. For a moment I thought he'd even give Mr. Patel a kiss or two, but luckily the doorman from my dad's building came forward and reached for our bags. I'd forgotten all about him.

"Just take those, please," I said, pointing to

the bags holding our pajamas and change of clothing. I held tight to the tote bag. I was wearing the woolen muffler that my grandmother had knitted me for Christmas, and I pulled it off and threw it on top of the tote bag. If Sammy tried to pop out, it might make it a little harder for him.

You can imagine how relieved I was when we were safely inside Dad's apartment.

The entire place, except for the kitchen and bathroom, is carpeted, so I knew that no one on the floor underneath would hear Sammy's feet pattering on the floor. And the kitchen and bathroom both had thick tile floors.

Dad admired Sammy. He also admired how I had managed to sneak him into the building right under the nose of the nosy doorman. "That guy knows everything about everyone in this place," he said to me.

So I felt pretty proud of my skill at hiding Sammy.

Sammy ran around the apartment, sniffing in all the corners and exploring under the bed and behind the curtains. Dad watched him. "He *is* trained, isn't he?" he wanted to know.

"I walked him just before we got into the taxi. And if we walk him at night, he should be okay."

"There's a different doorman at night," Dad observed. "So it shouldn't be a problem going in and out with the dog in the bag."

We called Mom, and Mitch told her all about the chicken man, which is what he called Mr. Patel. Dad said he'd drop us off on Sunday afternoon on his way to a late-afternoon concert he was going to.

At suppertime Dad said he'd discovered a new Chinese restaurant just a couple of blocks away. Mitch loves barbecued spareribs, and I love *everything* in a Chinese restaurant. Even tea. "Great!" I said, already imagining the taste of chicken fried rice and egg rolls.

I poured out Sammy's supper portion of

puppy food and a bowl of water too. Poor thing. I bet he'd love to gnaw on a sparerib bone or two. "We'll be back soon. Don't be lonely," I said, rubbing his back and giving him a good-bye hug. It's funny, I thought, that I never thought to say those same words to my mother when we left her.

The Golden Chopsticks turned out to be just as good as I'd hoped. I ate and ate until I was stuffed. Dad asked the usual questions about school, and Mitch told him all about Stephanie, the new girl who is in his day-care program. "She has red hair, and she's very pretty," he said.

"Aren't you a bit young to know if a girl is pretty or not?" Dad asked him.

"Nope," Mitch replied seriously. "Every-one knows when something is pretty or not. Spareribs aren't pretty. But they taste yummy. Stephanie is pretty."

"Well, don't take a bite out of her to find out if she's yummy," said Dad, laughing.

"Sammy bit Mom," Mitch reported, licking his fingers.

"What?" Dad asked.

"It was an accident," I said. "She pulled food away from him. Everyone knows you shouldn't do that."

"Hmm," said Dad. "Well, I hope it doesn't happen again."

"It won't," I promised him just as I had promised Mom.

We walked slowly back to Dad's building. Dad held Mitch's hand, and I walked along on the other side. I still hate everything about my parents' divorce, but this evening had turned out pretty well, I thought. There were no harsh words or bad feelings. If Mom had been along, she would have complained that the food was greasy or cost too much.

The good mood was broken at once as we reached Dad's building. "Mr. Wright," the doorman practically shouted as we entered the lobby. He was not the same man who had

seen Mitch and me when we arrived earlier. "What do you have in your apartment?"

"What do you mean, *what do I have*?" Dad asked, puzzled.

"You have a dog in there, don't you? It's been barking for the last hour. Several tenants have phoned me with complaints."

Dad's apartment is on the tenth floor. We couldn't hear anything until we reached the sixth floor, but from there on up Sammy came through loud and clear.

"Something must have frightened him," I said. "He never barks like this."

"He barked in the taxi," Mitch said.

"That's different. He was in the bag."

There was a message on Dad's answering machine from the president of the co-op board of his building. I listened as Dad played it through: "Mr. Wright. You know perfectly well that pets are not permitted in this building. You signed an agreement to that fact when you moved in here. I expect that animal to leave immediately. Otherwise you'll have to leave yourself."

That animal had stopped barking the moment we walked in the door. I'll never know what set him off. He wagged his tail happily and licked my hands when I petted him. I suppose Mom would have said he was enjoying the flavor of Chinese food on my fingers, but I knew it was because he was so overjoyed to see me again.

"I guess he was lonely in this strange place," I said, trying to excuse Sammy's behavior.

Dad got on the phone and spent the next ten minutes explaining that the dog in question was just a temporary houseguest. "It won't happen again. I promise you that," he said. It wasn't enough for the person on the other end because he continued talking for some time. At first Dad responded slowly and calmly, but as the man on the other end of the phone continued, my father's voice became louder and angrier. I shuddered at the sound. I had already forgotten what it was like when my parents had an argument.

Because he'd been discovered, I didn't have to put Sammy inside the tote bag when he went for his evening walk. One woman in the elevator going down said, "Isn't he adorable? I'd love to have a dog, but my husband has too many allergies." But on the way up an older man said, "What's he doing here? Dogs aren't permitted in this building."

"He's just a visitor," I said. "Don't worry. He won't be coming back." I wondered how I'd solve the problem of Sammy the next time I came to visit Dad.

7

What Happened to Mitch

Considering how happily the weekend had started off, it was all downhill after Friday evening. Dad decided he couldn't leave Sammy alone in the apartment, so in the morning he took Mitch to a nearby playground and I stayed in the apartment with Sammy. That way we knew he wouldn't disturb the neighbors with his barking. Well, that was okay with me. I turned on the TV, and Sammy and I watched some dopey shows together. I liked sitting on the sofa with Sammy lying beside me and licking my face from time to time. But when Dad returned with Mitch, he insisted that Sammy belonged on the floor and not on the furniture.

In the afternoon we all (that meant Sammy too) went for a long walk to get some exercise. Boring! At least it was boring until Sammy gave an unexpected pull on his leash when he saw a dog he wanted to get to know better. I lost my hold on the leash, and Sammy ran after the dog, who wasn't on a leash at all. The two dogs kept the other owner and me running for about ten minutes. It was a big relief when I got hold of Sammy at last. I was pooped.

"Can we go back to the apartment now?" I begged Dad.

On the way back to Dad's place we passed a shoe store. I stopped to look in the window. "Do you need new sneaks?" Dad asked, looking down at my old ones.

I nodded and hoped that Mitch wouldn't blab about the meal Sammy had made of my sneaker at home. We couldn't take the dog inside the store, but I told Dad my size and pointed to the ones I wanted that were in the window. They were exactly like the ones Sammy had destroyed.

So that was one very good thing that happened over the weekend. In the evening we ate TV dinners and watched a video. What with the fuss about Sammy and the new sneakers that I'd just gotten, I knew better than to complain. Even though the spaghetti was all soft and mushy, instead of the way it is when Mom cooks it, and the movie too silly for me, I pretended that everything was just fine.

Mitch fell asleep in the middle, and Dad turned down the volume. "Sorry about the fuss with your dog," he said, rubbing my hair. "I told you dogs are more trouble than they're worth."

"Sammy's not too much trouble," I said. "The people here just made a stupid rule. What's wrong with having a dog in an apartment?"

Dad shrugged his shoulders. "Some

people think dogs don't belong in city apartments. They need room to run around and be free. It isn't good for them to be cooped up for hours and hours when their owners are off at work or school. Of course there's also the question of noise, like last night."

"Sammy was in a new place and all alone," I said, defending him.

Dad just shook his head.

"You and Mom want me to adjust. Well, Sammy will adjust too," I said.

"I know, pal," Dad said. His voice sounded a little sad, and I wondered if he was sorry about the divorce. But then right away he started fiddling with the remote and he found a movie with a big car chase for us to watch. Sammy, who was not allowed on the sofa, slept on my feet until my feet fell asleep too. Then I got off the sofa and sat on the floor. Sammy stirred and licked my face before he fell asleep again. I know Dad loves me, but he doesn't show it the way Sammy does.

I wore my new sneakers home, after throwing away the box they came in with my dad's garbage.

"I thought I remembered you wearing your old sneaks when you left here," Mom commented when Mitch and I were home again.

"My old ones are in the overnight case," I said.

"Oh. You took both pairs with you," she responded, explaining to herself the mystery of the new sneakers. I didn't correct her. I planned to dig out the ones inside my closet and throw them in the school trash bin.

Another week was about to begin.

At school Mrs. Richmond returned some reports that we had written in class on Friday. We'd been reading a book called *The Search for Delicious*, by Natalie Babbitt. It's all about a king who wants to know what tastes best in the world, and our assignment was to write about something that tasted delicious.

"I'm very proud of you," Mrs. Richmond said, handing my paper to me. "I knew you had it in you, but you've even surpassed my hopes."

There was a big red A on the top page.

"I'd like you to read it aloud to the class," Mrs. Richmond told me.

Instead of describing a hot fudge sundae or a pepperoni pizza, I'd written about Sammy eating my new sneaker. Since I'd been asleep during half of his meal, I had to make some of it up. I said how first he licked it all over and then he nibbled at it slowly before he crunched all his teeth into the toe of the sneaker, mixing the leather and rubber into a delicious blend of two textures and two flavors.

I could hear my classmates giggling at some of my comments, and when I finished, they burst into applause. I could hardly believe it.

"You're a real writer," Corey called out.

"I bet you could write a whole book," Dana added.

At that moment I felt as if I *could* write a whole book if I had something to write about.

As I was leaving school that afternoon, Mrs. Richmond stopped me for a moment. "I know you've had to adapt to the changes in your life," she said. "But I'm relieved that you're back on track again. You're one of my best students, and I was worried about you for a bit. If you need to talk to someone, please remember that I'll always be here for you."

I couldn't think of anything to say, so I just turned red and kind of shrugged my shoulders.

"I'm going to phone your mother and tell her what a great report you did."

Well, then I did have something to say. "Could you just not tell her the subject of it?" I begged.

For a moment Mrs. Richmond looked puzzled. Then she looked down at my feet and began laughing. "Oh, Curtis," she gasped between laughs. "You poor kid."

"It's okay now. Sort of," I said, hoping I wouldn't have to go into the whole story.

"I think I understand," said Mrs. Richmond. She gave me a hug. "Keep those sneakers away from your dog," she warned me.

"You don't have to tell me that," I said, grinning at her.

Mrs. Richmond phoned while I was walking Sammy, so I don't know exactly what she and my mother talked about. But since Mom had a huge smile on her face when we returned, I knew I didn't have to worry.

Mitch was in bed, one arm around his teddy bear and half-asleep, when I tiptoed into the room to get my library book. Seeing me, he sat up. "I need to make peepee," he announced.

"Okay, come on," I said, knowing that it's important for him to make it to the toilet right away when he has to go. Also, if he went now, he'd probably stay dry through the night.

The teddy dropped out of Mitch's arm and onto the floor as he left the room.

I was searching through my backpack for the library book, so I didn't see Mitch come back into the room. Suddenly I heard a terrible scream.

I swung around and immediately realized what had happened. Sammy had taken the teddy bear in his mouth, and Mitch had tried to grab it away.

"What is it?" my mother shouted as she ran into the bedroom.

She picked up Mitch and hugged him. "What happened, baby? Why are you crying?"

I winced. One of the things my parents used to fight about was the way my mother always called Mitch her baby. "He's three years old now," my father would say.

But Mitch's sobs sure sounded like a baby's.

"Did Sammy scare you?" Mom asked my brother.

She looked down at his hands and let out a scream of her own. That made Mitch cry even harder.

Sammy ran around and around in the room with the teddy bear in his mouth. He didn't understand all the commotion.

"Look. He's bleeding. Sammy bit him," Mom said.

"Where?" I asked. I refused to believe it. Mitch had wanted his teddy, and he was upset that Sammy had taken it.

"What's this?" my mother asked.

Mitch's thumb was wet and red. It could be only one thing.

Mom took Mitch into the bathroom and ran cold water on his hand. She let him pick out the bandage he wanted from a box of kiddie strips that have pictures on them, and she washed his face. Then, sitting on the closed toilet seat, she rocked him in her arms for a long time.

Meanwhile I calmed Sammy down and, distracting him with a slice of bologna from my next day's lunch, I got the teddy bear away from him.

I brought the toy into the bathroom and held it out to Mitch. His eyes were red and half closed with sleep. His body heaved with soft sobs, but he reached for his bear.

When he had fallen asleep, my mother carried him to his bed. I was sitting in the living room pretending to read my library book.

She came into the room and plopped down on the sofa. I could see that she was tired.

"It was an accident," I told her. "Mitch got scared, but he didn't get really badly hurt."

"Oh, Curtis, it's not that simple," she said, turning toward me. "I know you want to keep Sammy, but we just can't."

"He won't do it again," I said.

"I wish I could believe that," Mom said. "But he bit me, and now he's bitten your brother. We can't keep a dog like that. I warned you that if it happened again, he'd have to go. Tomorrow, when I get home from work, we'll take Sammy back to the animal shelter. Maybe some other family can deal with him. But we can't."

"What are you doing? Divorcing him, like you divorced Dad? If you don't like someone, you just throw them out of your life, don't you?" I said angrily.

"You can't compare a dog with a human being," my mother said. "We'll wait awhile, and maybe in a few months we can look for another dog."

"I don't want another dog. I want Sammy," I said. Then I added, "If Sammy goes, I go too. He's my dog and my best friend. You can't just get rid of him like that."

"Oh, Curtis," my mother said, "Sammy's your dog, but Mitchell's your brother. And I'm your mother. That dog has bitten us both."

"It wasn't Sammy's fault," I said. "Mitch shouldn't have grabbed the teddy from him."

"Mitch is three years old. This time Sammy nipped his thumb. Who knows what could happen next time? But there isn't going to be a next time."

I started to say something, but my mother interrupted. "Go to bed now," she said. "There's nothing we can do tonight. Thank goodness we know that Sammy doesn't have rabies. And Mitch had a tetanus booster not too long ago."

Sammy started to follow me into the bedroom, but Mom grabbed his collar and shut him in the kitchen. "He's not going anywhere near Mitch," she told me.

I was so upset about losing Sammy that I couldn't sleep. I lay in bed thinking of wild schemes. I'd said it, and I meant it. If Sammy went, so would I. We'd run away together. I just had to figure out how and where.

8

Leaving Home

I guess I fell asleep after all because I remember waking up. I turned in bed and missed the warm bump that in less than two weeks I had come to expect. For a moment I was too groggy to realize what was wrong, and then I sat up with a start. Sammy was not in my bed, and if my mother had her way, he would be out of my life in a few hours.

I got out of bed and tiptoed into the kitchen. It wasn't totally dark because we don't have a curtain on the window, and the streetlight shines in. Quiet as I was, Sammy woke at once. I heard his paws scratching on the linoleum as he rushed toward me. I sat on the floor and hugged him hard. "Sammy," I whispered, "what am I going to do?"

Of course he couldn't answer. Instead he licked my face. I wanted to take him back to bed with me, but I knew my mother would have a fit if she discovered him there in the morning. So I did the next best thing. I went back to my bed and got my comforter and pillow and brought them into the kitchen. I put half the comforter under my body and used the other half to cover myself. Sammy curled up beside me and was quickly asleep again.

I lay awake, thinking and planning. I was going to run away. But where and how? I had seventeen dollars and change in an envelope underneath my T-shirts in the drawer in the bedroom. I knew that there was more than two hundred dollars in my bank account. My great-aunt sends a check for ten dollars for my birthday and Christmas every year, and my mother insisted that a savings account was something everyone needs. I'd never thought it was a good plan before. Now I was relieved to know that there would be plenty of money for Sammy and me.

But where would we go? I couldn't go to my father. My grandparents live in Florida. I'd never been there. They usually come to New York for a couple of weeks each spring. I wondered how they'd feel if I suddenly showed up in Sarasota with a dog. What would I say? "This is your granddog. We've run away." I wondered how much it would cost to go to Florida. How long would it take?

I thought about Danny at my old apartment building. I'd go and stay with him except his mother was allergic to dogs. Danny really envied my having a dog. He knew he could never get one until he was a grown-up.

The refrigerator motor clicked on, startling me, and Sammy shifted in his sleep. "Oh, Sammy, Sammy, Sammy . . . ," I whispered to him in the half dark.

Suddenly I had another idea. I'd go stay

with my old friend Sammy Eisenberg. Connecticut was a whole lot closer than Florida. It would be lots cheaper to travel there. Sammy lived in West—West—Westport. Or was it Weston . . . or Westbury? It was something like that. I knew my mom had written it down in her address book.

Wouldn't Sammy be amazed to see me after so many years? Wouldn't he be surprised that I named my dog after him? I wondered if he would recognize me. Did he still remember the day the two of us got lost in Central Park? It had been only for ten minutes, but being four years old, we had thought it was at least an hour. I remembered how the two of us walked through the park, holding hands, not talking to strangers. We both were scared to death as we went looking for our mothers, who were busy sitting and talking on a park bench and didn't even know we had walked away.

The refrigerator motor went off, and the

kitchen was quiet. I lay back on my pillow and imagined the two Sammys, the boy and the dog, and me running around in that big yard in Connecticut. I had visited there only once, but it had made a strong impression on me.

"What in the world do you think you're doing?" a voice shouted at me.

I rubbed my eyes and looked up. My mother was standing over me. She was wearing her bathrobe, and her hair stuck out all over.

What was I doing on the kitchen floor?

Then Sammy came over and licked my face, and I remembered everything.

"Since you wouldn't let Sammy sleep in the bedroom with me, I came and slept with him," I said angrily.

"Listen, Curtis," my mother said, using her I'm-trying-hard-to-be-patient-with-you voice. "I don't want any scenes or fusses. Take your bedding and go into your room. You have to get ready for school."

"What about Sammy?" I asked hopefully. Maybe she'd had a change of heart during the night. Maybe she would give Sammy another chance and I wouldn't have to run away with him.

"You know *what about Sammy*," she said softly. "He's got to go. I'm really sorry about it, but there's no other way."

"He's very gentle," I argued. "He didn't mean to bite Mitch."

"Curtis, I'm as much to blame as Sammy," my mother said. "I acted too hastily when I agreed to let you have a dog. Maybe that's the root of all my problems. Acting hastily. Your father and I got married within three months of meeting each other. Important steps should take more time and more thought."

"Don't compare getting a dog with getting married," I said angrily as I stood up and started toward the bedroom with my pillow and comforter.

"Do you want to see my boo-boo?"

Mitchell asked me from his bed. He was busy peeling back his bandage to admire the small red mark underneath.

"Nope."

I opened the closet and pulled out my warm corduroy slacks. I put on a turtleneck shirt and a heavy sweater on top. Mom was behind with the laundry, so there wasn't a whole lot of extra underwear in my drawer. But after I was all dressed, there were still two more pairs of socks and underwear. I took my school things out of my backpack and stuffed in a couple of T-shirts and the clean underwear. I counted out the seventeen dollars and forty-five cents and put them into the zipper pocket on the side.

"You're rich," my brother said when he saw my money.

"No, I'm not," I replied.

"Could I have just one?" he begged.

I looked at him sitting in his fuzzy red pj's. Who knew when I'd ever see him again? I unzipped the pocket and took out a one-dollar bill. Sixteen dollars would be more than enough for a ticket to Connecticut. Besides, I also had my bankbook, which would get me the rest of my money.

"Put it away," I told him. "Save it for something special. Maybe Dad will take you to that new toy store. You could get a huge bottle of bubbles with this."

Mitch jumped off his bed and hugged my legs, which was as high as he could reach.

"Where are you going?" he wanted to know.

"I'm going away with Sammy."

"Away? Can I come too?"

That struck me as funny. Here I was, getting ready to run away with my dog so he wouldn't bite my brother, and my brother wanted to join us.

"Nope."

"That's okay. I have to go to Mrs. Joyce now anyway," said Mitch.

Mrs. Joyce is the woman at the day-care

center who takes care of him while Mom is at work.

When I went into the kitchen, Sammy was just licking up the last crumb of his breakfast chow.

"Take him for his walk, and I'll have some scrambled eggs waiting for you when you get back," Mom said.

Sure enough, there was the warm, good smell of bacon, eggs, and toast in the kitchen when I came back upstairs with Sammy. Bacon! Mom never makes bacon in the middle of the week. It takes too long and is too messy to clean up. She was trying to make me feel better. Well, it wasn't going to work. But I knew I should eat a good, big breakfast while I could.

Mom was in the bedroom getting Mitchell ready for day care. They came into the kitchen just as Sammy finished the slice of bacon I'd sneaked to him. He licks his lips for about ten minutes after eating, so Mom knew right away what I'd done. But for once she didn't say anything about it.

"We'll take Sammy to the shelter this afternoon," she said. "I'm sure they'll find another home for him. A place where he can run around and be happy."

"But you don't care if I'm not happy, do you?" I asked accusingly.

"Curtis, don't say things like that," Mom said, shaking her head. "I do care about your happiness. It means everything to me. But we just can't keep an animal that bites people. So he's got to go."

"And I'm going too," I told her.

"Oh, honey." She reached out to hug me.

I backed away. "Sammy and I won't be here when you get home from work," I announced.

I picked up my lunch bag from the kitchen counter, and I marched out of the kitchen and into the bedroom. I pushed the lunch into my backpack, and then I looked around the room that Mitch and I had been sharing. Was there anything else I should take with me? Amazingly, the one thing that sort of jumped out at me was Mitch's teddy bear. I should have hated that old bear. If Mitch hadn't dropped it last night and if Sammy hadn't taken it and if Mitch hadn't tried to get it back, nothing would have happened. But looking at that old worn bear, I just felt sad. I knew I was going to miss my little brother.

I returned to the kitchen and took my jacket off the back of the chair where I'd hung it. Then, suddenly remembering, I got the canvas tote bag out of the hall closet. It would come in handy when Sammy and I boarded the train. A bag, half full of puppy chow, was on the kitchen counter. I picked it up and put it inside my backpack. Now I'd taken everything I'd need. I was ready to go.

"Come on, Sammy," I called, holding his leash.

Sammy gave a happy bark. He couldn't

believe his good luck. He'd already had a morning walk. This was the time when everyone left him all alone in the house. Instead I was offering him a second chance to go exploring.

"You really think you're going away with that dog?" my mom asked.

"Yep."

I bent over and gave Mitch a hug. "So long, Mitchie," I said. "Blow a bubble for me."

Mitch grinned at our secret.

"Curtis," my mother shrieked.

I had been about to give her a good-bye hug too. Who knew when I'd see her again? But the way she was acting, I knew I'd better just leave and leave fast.

"We'll be in touch," I called as Sammy and I went out the door.

"Curtis, wait—"

The door slammed between us as Sammy and I ran down the three flights of stairs to the street. Unlike my father, we have no elevator and no doorman in our building. That made our getaway simpler—no waiting for the elevator to take us down to the street, no suspicious looks from someone wondering what I was up to.

My plan had been to stop at the bank and then go on to Grand Central Station. The weather was cold but clear. It was a walk of only thirty or so blocks. They say that twenty city blocks is equal to a mile. So what's a mile-and-a-half walk when you're running away? But suddenly I thought my mom might come after me. So when an empty taxi stopped at the corner for the light, I grabbed the door handle and climbed inside with Sammy. At least that was one thing I learned from the divorce. How to nab a New York City taxicab like a pro!

I sat down and told the driver my destination. I saw my mom and Mitch running down the street, but they didn't see me.

I was really sharp, I thought.

Then I remembered something. I had forgotten to copy down Sammy Eisenberg's address from Mom's address book.

9

The Third Time

There was only one thing I could do. I wasn't sure of the town, much less the street name, where I was headed. So I told the driver to take me back home.

It's a pretty common sight to see kids riding in taxis in New York, so I'm sure the driver didn't suspect that I was running away. He didn't make any snide comments like "What's the matter kid, cold feet?" Instead he just turned at the next corner, and five minutes after I'd left home, I was back again.

I thought of asking him to wait for me but realized that now that my mother was out of sight, I didn't need a taxi anymore. So I paid the three-dollar fare and sighed about being stupid enough to waste so much of my money. But after all, I'd never run away before. So I guess I should have expected that I'd make a mistake or two.

Sammy climbed up the stairs with me. Going up three flights is never as much fun as running down. I didn't remove his leash, just dropped it as I rushed to check out my mom's address book. I flipped the pages until I found the name "Eisenberg" and the address "181 Whippoorwill Lane, Westport, CT."

I remember how Sammy's mother had told me that whippoorwills were birds, but that they'd never seen one since they'd moved in. Perhaps by now they had. I didn't bother to write the address down. I knew I'd remember it.

I hurried back into the kitchen and found Sammy happily chewing up the remains of the package of bacon. I didn't care that there wouldn't be any left for Mom and Mitch, but I was sure that raw bacon could make him really sick.

"Hey, Sammy," I said, making a dive for the chewed-up package, "don't eat that."

Suddenly there was a sharp, burning pain in my hand. It took me a minute to realize what had happened. Sammy had bitten me, just the way he'd bitten my mother and Mitchell. Only this time, instead of a trickle of blood, it was pouring out like a faucet. I grabbed a kitchen towel to mop it up.

"Sammy, how could you do this to me?" I wailed as I tried to clean up the floor with a corner of the towel. But the more I tried to clean up, the more blood spurted out of my hand onto the floor. It was on my pants and my jacket too. And the pain in my hand was so bad I could hardly move my fingers.

I sat down on the floor and began crying. How could I have been so dumb? How could Sammy have been so mean?

It's hard for me to believe, but I think I passed out. Just the way people do in the movies. I don't think I lost that much blood. Anyhow, the next thing I knew, my mom was there leaning over me and patting my head with a damp washcloth.

"Where's Mitch?" I asked her.

"Shh," she said. "He's at day care."

"Good." I didn't want Mitch to get scared seeing me on the floor surrounded by so much blood. He would be afraid of dogs for the next hundred years.

"Why did you come back?" Mom asked.

"I needed Sammy Eisenberg's address," I said. "I'm going there to live with him."

But even as I said it, I knew I was no longer going away. How could I take my dog there? Maybe he'd bite my old friend. Maybe he'd bite his sister. Maybe he'd bite me again on the train.

"Can you stand up?" Mom asked.

"Sure," I said, but discovered that it wasn't so easy.

"I'm taking you over to the emergency

room at the hospital. I think you may need stitches."

"Stitches?" I'd never had stitches before.

We took another taxi, and sure enough, I got six small stitches at the hospital. I was a little scared, but the doctor gave me a shot that totally numbed my hand so I didn't feel anything. The bodies of the nurse and the doctor blocked my view, so I couldn't see the actual sewing. But when the doctor was finished, I saw the stitches, done with black thread. Then the nurse wrapped my hand in a bandage to protect it and keep it clean.

"You'll have to come back in about ten days to have the stitches removed," the doctor explained to me as she gave me a tetanus shot because my mother couldn't remember when I'd had my last one.

When we got back to the apartment, I was surprised to see my dad waiting outside for us.

"I called him," Mom explained as we all

slowly walked up the stairs.

"Hey, pal," Dad said, looking at my bandaged hand. "I know you don't like to do your homework, but wasn't that an extreme solution to get out of it?"

I knew he was joking, so I tried to smile, but I began crying at the same time.

"He didn't even cry when he had the stitches," Mom told Dad.

"It just shows how bad my jokes are," my father said.

"I'm crying because of Sammy," I explained.

"We know," Dad said.

He looked as if he might start crying too. "Would it help if I took the dog back to the shelter for you?" he asked Mom.

Mom turned to me.

"Okay," I said. "But you must make them promise that they won't hurt him." I paused for a moment. "And I have to say good-bye to him before he goes."

Mom and Dad left me alone in the kitchen with Sammy. "Sammy," I said, "my dad is going to take you to the shelter. Maybe they can find another place for you. But you've got to behave. It's wrong to bite people. Wrong. Wrong. Wrong. Look what you did to me." I held out my bandaged hand so he could get a good look.

Only the tips of my fingers stuck out, but Sammy came over to lick them. For a second I was afraid to let him near my hand, but his pink tongue licked me so gently that it was hard to imagine that only a couple of hours before, his teeth had crunched down on that same hand.

So that's the story of how I had a dog and had to give him up. But there's one more thing: When Dad took Sammy away, he had an idea. He didn't tell me about it because he wasn't sure it would work out. One of the men he works with lives outside the city in a house that was once part of a farm. There's

a lot of land, and the man and his wife love dogs. They already had two. Dad spoke with them, and they agreed to take Sammy.

"He's going to be very happy there, and they're going to train him not to snap and bite," Dad told me after it was all arranged.

When Mitch came home from school and saw my bandaged hand, I think he was a little jealous. His Band-Aids were awfully small compared with my bandage. But in the evening, when it was bedtime and I didn't have Sammy curling up next to me in bed, he did the most amazing thing. He climbed out of his bed, and he handed me his teddy.

"You can sleep with him tonight," he said.

You know what? I did.

Mom had to write a note to Mrs. Richmond about why I was absent. She didn't write about the running-away part, but she did say my dog had bitten me and we'd had to give him up.

"Curtis," Mrs. Richmond said, "I think

you should write a story about it. Tell every bit of what happened and how you felt. Put in all the details, just the way you did when you described Sammy eating your sneaker. That's what real writers do. And you're a writer. I don't say that to all my students. In fact I've only said it once before in my career."

"Who did you say it to last time?" I asked her.

She leaned over and whispered a name to me.

"Really? Was he in your class?" I asked, amazed. She'd told me the name of one of the most popular writers in the library.

"Don't tell anyone," she begged me. "I don't like name-dropping."

"I don't even have a picture of Sammy," I told Mrs. Richmond. "He was with us such a short time, I didn't get a chance to take his picture."

"You'll have his picture in words when

you're done," she told me. "It will be even better than a snapshot."

Anyway, that's why I'm writing all about Sammy. I mostly hate sad stories, and this is a sad one. But you know, that's how life is: happy and sad.

"You learned a lot earlier than I did that life doesn't end happily ever after," Mom said.

"But life isn't over," I reminded her.

My parents may never get back together again. But I know that someday I'm going to get another dog. In the meantime Dad's promised to take Mitch and me to visit Sammy on some of the weekends we spend together. It's not the same as having a dog of my own, but it's better than nothing. Besides, even though he bit me, I still love Sammy.

Oh, one other thing. Mom told me that she hadn't crossed out the Eisenbergs' address in our book but that just a few weeks ago in the supermarket, she met someone who had also known them when they lived in New York City.

"Guess what?" the woman had said to Mom. "Remember the Eisenbergs who used to live on Seventy-fifth Street? I just heard that Greg Eisenberg's company transferred him. They've moved to Seattle."

I think it's pretty lucky that I went back home for their address and got bitten by Sammy. Otherwise I might be walking up and down the streets in Westport, Connecticut, from now until next Christmas, looking for someone who doesn't even live there anymore.

Last weekend when Mitch and I went to visit Dad, he had some presents for us. Mitch got two plastic dinosaurs. Dad gave me half a dozen paperback books. "These are all great dog stories that I think you'll enjoy," he said. "After all, outside of a dog, a book is man's best friend. And inside a dog it's too dark to read."

It took a second for the words to sink in.

"Oh, Dad," I groaned. "That's even worse than your usual jokes."

My father shrugged. "Sorry, pal," he apologized. "But at least I can't claim any credit for that one. I'm quoting Groucho Marx."

I don't know who Groucho Marx is. I guess he never owned and had to give up a dog like Sammy. If he had, he wouldn't have made up a corny joke like that.

Still, I've already read one of the books from my dad. And I'll read the others too. But when I finish writing all I remember about Sammy, I hope it will be better than any of them. Because as dogs go, my one small dog was the best.

WHAT WENT WRONG?

Every year millions of people acquire dogs. Most of them develop happy, loving relationships with their pets. What went wrong in this story?

Owning a dog is a big commitment. It's a commitment of daily time, caring, and energy, and it's also a commitment in years. You should remember when you get a dog that you are acquiring a pet that may live for the next fifteen or more years. Therefore, no one should act impulsively. Much thought should be given to the decision. Curtis wanted a dog, and his mother impulsively gave in. They should both have done some serious research before the selection was made.

It is certainly possible to get a fine and healthy dog from an animal shelter. But you should look around and give the matter thought. Curtis's eye quickly landed on a cute dog and he stopped looking and considering other possibilities.

Some dogs that are underweight become very aggressive around and protective of their food. Perhaps this was Sammy's problem. More likely, however, without any training, he just did whatever he wanted. Curtis's mother couldn't handle the situation, and neither could Curtis.

Curtis needed to teach Sammy the basic commands of *sit*, *stay*, *heel*, *come*, and *down* to gain his dog's respect. It takes patience, knowledge, determination, and love to train a dog. Unfortunately, poor Curtis was equipped only with love, and it was not enough. Had he received professional help from a dog trainer or taken a dog training class, Curtis could have avoided the heartbreak of giving up Sammy. Dog training classes are frequently given at community centers or through general education programs. There are also books and videos available to help a new dog owner.

We can hope that, someday in the future, Curtis will get another chance to own a dog.

—Larry Berg
Certified Professional Dog Trainer
and Behaviorist
Creator of the video *Train Your Dog
before Your Dog Trains You!*
American Kennel Club Judge